HORSE DIARIES
· Golden Sun ·

HORSE DIARIES

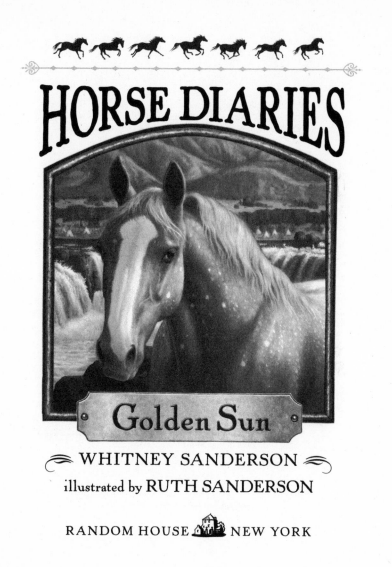

Golden Sun

WHITNEY SANDERSON

illustrated by RUTH SANDERSON

RANDOM HOUSE NEW YORK

Text copyright © 2010 by Whitney Robinson
Illustrations copyright © 2010 by Ruth Sanderson
Photograph on p. 135 © Ruth Sanderson

All rights reserved. Published in the United States by Random House
Children's Books, a division of Random House, Inc., New York.

Random House and the colophon are registered trademarks of Random House, Inc.

Visit us on the Web! www.randomhouse.com/kids

Educators and librarians, for a variety of teaching tools, visit us at
www.randomhouse.com/teachers

Library of Congress Cataloging-in-Publication Data
Sanderson, Whitney.
Golden Sun / by Whitney Sanderson ; illustrated by Ruth Sanderson. — 1st ed.
p. cm. — (Horse diaries)
Summary: Follows Golden Sun, an Appaloosa horse, through several seasons
as Little Turtle, a Nez Perce boy, raises and trains him then takes him along on a
vision quest in hopes of saving his friend Pale Moon from serious illness.
ISBN 978-0-375-86194-9 (trade) — ISBN 978-0-375-96194-6 (lib. bdg.) —
ISBN 978-0-375-89348-3 (e-book)
1. Appaloosa horse—Juvenile fiction. 2. Nez Percé Indians—Juvenile fiction.
[1. Appaloosa horse—Fiction. 2. Horses—Fiction. 3. Nez Percé Indians—Fiction.
4. Shamans—Fiction. 5. Indians of North America—Northwest, Pacific—Fiction.
6. Northwest, Pacific—History—Fiction.] I. Sanderson, Ruth, ill. II. Title.
PZ10.3.R5913Gol 2010 [Fic]—dc22 2009026562

Printed in the United States of America

10 9 8 7

First Edition

CONTENTS

"Oh! if people knew what a comfort to horses a light hand is . . ."
—from *Black Beauty*, by Anna Sewell

HORSE DIARIES
·Golden Sun·

The Salmon Falls,
Oregon, 1790

A sound like thunder filled my ears, though the sky was bright and blue. The earth trembled under my hooves. I pressed close to the horses around me for comfort. Sweat ran down our dusty flanks, and our eyes were white-rimmed and wild.

The men drove us down into the roaring valley. They kept us packed tightly together so we couldn't turn and bolt back the way we came. As we drew closer, I realized the sound was made by water. More water than I had ever seen in my life. It foamed like spit around an angry dog's mouth, plunging down the rocks to the river below. I wanted to run from the sound, but I was afraid to leave the safety of the herd.

"*Tawts*, Golden Sun." The familiar voice sounded small and far away among the whinnies of horses and the crash of the waterfall. I craned my neck and saw Little Turtle riding toward me on one of his father's horses, a gray mare named Sparrow.

I paused while they threaded their way among the crush of horses to reach my side. Little Turtle leaned down to stroke my neck. He was nine winters old, and had cared for me since I was born last *Latit'al*, the season of new life.

Little Turtle's father was a respected warrior who owned many horses. He had promised his son a foal to train, and Little Turtle chose me. Although the waterfall buzzed like a swarm of angry bees, I trusted that Little Turtle would not lead me toward harm. Trying to shake the sound of the roaring water from my ears, I lowered my head and followed Sparrow and Little Turtle into the valley.

As we drew closer, the wind blew cold spray from the waterfall into our faces. On the far side of the river, a vast, barren plain stretched away to hazy mountains on the horizon. Both sides of the riverbank were lined with tepees, and many strange people were setting up their tepees, tending to their horses, and cooking their dinners. Some dressed differently from my people, the *Nimi'ipuu*, and spoke different words. Sparrow once told me a story of how she met a stallion here who said his grandsire had come from a distant place called Spain, where the land was hardly visible for all the people and horses and lodges crowded upon it. The stallion's grandsire had been put on a boat that sailed for months and months across a river that seemed to go on in all directions without end.

Sparrow was so excited when she told the story that I did not say anything, but I think the stallion was probably making it up. I could not imagine water bigger or more furious than the raging waterfall in front of me.

As the wind continued to blow, the oily scent of fish filled my nostrils. I didn't like the way it smelled, but I knew that salmon was an important source of food to the *Nimi'ipuu*. I knew how vital it was to gather enough food before *Haoq'oy*, the cold season. I shivered as I remembered the long months of my first winter, huddled close to my dam as she foraged for dried grass and bark stripped from the trees.

Now dozens of men milled about on wooden platforms over the river. They filled their nets with shimmering red and silver salmon. When we reached an open place for his family to set up camp, Little Turtle put leather hobbles around my front legs to keep me from wandering off. Nearby, other families in Little Turtle's tribe began to set up their homes.

Already strange men and women were wandering over to appraise the horses. Everyone knew the *Nimi'ipuu* had the best horses. My tribe called spotted horses like me *Maamin*. Not every *Nimi'ipuu* horse had spots, and the birth of a beautifully marked foal was a particular cause for excitement.

Among the unfamiliar people, I saw two who were unlike anyone I had ever seen. They had bushy red hair growing like lichen from their chins, and they wore hats made from raccoon skins with the tail hanging down the back. Their eyes were blue as robins' eggs. One of them pointed at me.

"Look at the spots on that one," he said. "I'll bet he's fast, too. They say a Palouse pony is worth ten ordinary ponies in a race."

Their words were as much of a mystery as their strange appearance. The rhythm of their speech sounded different from Little Turtle's. I perked up my ears as one of them offered me something on his hand. It was a flat red and white stick. I sniffed it curiously. It smelled sweet, and that was enough of an invitation for me! I crunched down on the stick. It tasted sweet as maple sap, with a tangy flavor like the wintergreen berries that grew in shady forests during the late gathering-time of *Hoplal*.

I wanted to keep the wonderful taste in my mouth forever, but soon it dissolved away to nothing. The strange men moved on with the others, and Little Turtle's family paused now and then to greet old friends as they stretched buffalo hides across their tepee frame.

As they worked, I watched the strange horses scattered across the river valley. The *Nimi'ipuu* traded away many of their horses, and I hoped to see someone I knew. I scanned the herds for the familiar brown-and-white spotted coat of my dam. Little Turtle's father had traded her to another tribe last *Q'oyxt'sal*, right after I was weaned. I was disappointed when I didn't see her among the campsites.

I knew all the families would hold games and horseback races later on, and I wished I were old enough to join in. But I was only a yearling, and Little Turtle knew better than to ride me before I was fully grown. He had learned a lot from his father, and I thought he understood horses better than many grown men.

Little Turtle's gestures and tone of voice were clear, and he did not get angry if I didn't understand something right away. I often forgot we spoke different languages, because Little Turtle seemed part horse.

When the evening's work was done, Little Turtle came over to rub the sweat from my coat with a soft deerskin cloth. He leaned down and blew softly into my nose in greeting as he wiped away the dust that had crusted around my eyes and mouth. Then he picked up a sharp rock and scraped the dirt from my hooves.

Little Turtle's friend Pale Moon came over as he worked. She was also nine winters old, and her family and Little Turtle's were like kin.

"Golden Sun is looking well," said Pale Moon as Little Turtle ran his fingers through my tail to pick out a few stray burrs.

"Thank you," replied Little Turtle. "I can't wait until he is old enough to ride! Can you imagine how wonderful it will be when we can gallop together across the prairie, racing the hawks?"

Pale Moon cast her eyes down and bit her lip. Though I did not understand most of the words they spoke, I wondered if they were talking about Foxtail. The bay mare had been Pale Moon's horse since she was small, but she had died foaling this spring.

"I wish I had a horse who was as dear to me as Golden Sun is to you," said Pale Moon. "Now I just ride whichever of my father's horses I can catch most easily. I do not feel the same connection to them that I felt to Foxtail."

Little Turtle nodded sympathetically. "My father is letting me ride Sparrow until Golden Sun is grown, but I do not feel she is really my horse. Don't worry, I am sure that in time you will find a horse who is as special to you as Foxtail was."

Pale Moon smiled sadly, then went off to help her mother put her young sister to bed. The light began to fade from the sky. I was sure

Little Turtle was tired from the day's journey, but he stayed watching me as dusk gathered. Soon I could see only his slender silhouette in the darkness. I wondered if maybe he had fallen asleep on his feet like a horse.

Then Little Turtle reached out to run his fingers through my mane. He took his obsidian knife from his belt and cut away a golden lock of my hair. He tucked it into the turtle-shell

pouch around his neck. The shell was almost the size of his fist, with leather sewn around the edges to turn it into a bag. Other members of the tribe wore these pouches also, although most were woven or made from leather. They called them medicine bags.

I had seen Little Turtle put other things in his medicine bag before. Several months earlier, he had met a Cayuse family in the camas fields. Little Turtle had traded the skin of a rabbit he caught for a beautiful glass bead that glinted with rainbow colors.

Another time when we were walking by the river, Little Turtle had found a very round white stone with a crack down the middle, like a hatching egg. He had put that in his turtle-shell bag, too. As Little Turtle tucked my lock of hair into his bag, I understood that it contained things that were special to him.

Little Turtle's mother finally called him to bed, and he followed her into his family's tepee. I was tired also, and I soon fell asleep despite the neighs of strange horses and the embers of many dying fires swirling on the breeze.

Runaway

The next morning, Little Turtle and his father, Sitting Bear, went out on one of the platforms at the edge of the river and hauled nets full of glistening salmon from the water. Little Turtle's mother cleaned the salmon by cutting out their insides and stripping off the scales. She set them to dry on racks in the sun.

When evening came, the tribes feasted and played games together. Little Turtle led me over to watch the races. The winners took home many prizes: beaded jewelry, cedarwood bows, buffalo overcoats, even the horses of losing riders.

A man on a fiery pinto stallion was win-ning everything in sight. When a new rider came forward to challenge him, the man laughed and the stallion tossed his foaming head as if he were laughing, too. Although he was steaming and lathered from his many races, the stallion swept past every competitor until there were none left undefeated.

Then, to my surprise, the man jumped off his horse and came over to where Little Turtle and I were standing. "A fine-looking colt," he said. He looked me up and down. "Sturdy legs, tough feet, a well-formed neck and head."

Little Turtle nodded his thanks.

"His coat is striking," the man continued. "Like snow dappled on golden earth. What do you want for him?"

Before Little Turtle could answer, Sitting Bear came over. He and his favorite stallion, Fire Tail, had just lost a race to the stranger. Sitting Bear was still breathing heavily from the race, and Fire Tail was lathered with sweat.

"What business do you have with my son, White Eagle?" Sitting Bear said. His tone was polite, but I could hear a trace of resentment beneath. He had just lost one of his good mares in the race. On the other side of the

campsite, I could see White Eagle's children fussing over the blue roan mare we had called Dream Seeker.

"I was wondering if that colt he's holding is for trade," White Eagle said.

"What are you offering?" said Sitting Bear.

Although I could not understand their words, I could tell from their gazes that they were discussing me. I pawed the ground lightly and arched my neck.

White Eagle brought forward some of the spoils he had won that day: a finely carved bow and arrow set, some woven sacks of food, and a deerskin shirt decorated with colorful glass beads, porcupine quills, and feathers.

From the glint in Sitting Bear's eye, I knew White Eagle had just made a good offer. Sitting

Bear was a fair man, but he did not get attached to his horses. I still remembered the first lonely nights after my dam had been traded away.

Sitting Bear's eyes seemed to reflect the shine of the glass beads. Little Turtle looked anxious. Was I about to be traded away from him for the price of some supplies and a pretty shirt?

Sitting Bear looked to White Eagle, to the offering, and then to his wide-eyed son. "That is a very generous offer for an unbroken colt," he said finally. "But this is Little Turtle's horse, and it is his decision whether to accept the trade."

Little Turtle put a possessive hand on my neck. "Golden Sun is not for sale," he said.

White Eagle nodded, looking disappointed, and gathered his things. I breathed a sigh of relief and lowered my head.

Sitting Bear glanced at his son. "That would have been a fine trade for a decorated warhorse, much less a weanling colt," he said.

"Golden Sun is my friend," Little Turtle replied. "I could not place a value on him."

Sitting Bear showed little expression as he led his tired horse away to the river for a drink. I could not tell if he was pleased or angry. Little Turtle turned to me, his face showing relief also.

He began to work with me, as he often did in his spare moments, teaching me to accept touch and to respond to the cues of his voice and body. Little Turtle ran his hands across my face, my ears, my flanks, and my belly. His light touch sometimes felt like a fly landing on me, but I had learned not to stamp my hooves and twitch his hand from my skin.

Little Turtle squeezed my leg just above the knee, over the hard chestnut, to make me lift my hoof. I felt unbalanced with only three feet on the ground. I tried to pull my hoof away, but Little Turtle held it steady until I relaxed.

Little Turtle began trimming my hoof with his obsidian knife. It didn't hurt, but I disliked the feeling of the knife scraping against the hard sole of my foot. Still, I knew I would be able to run more freely when my hooves were trimmed.

As we worked, Little Turtle's friend Pale

Moon came over to watch. Little Turtle took his training cloth from his belt. I knew that when he had the piece of soft leather in his hand, it was time for me to pay attention. He held the cloth loosely by his side and began to walk away with swinging strides, gazing off into the distance. He looked like he was going somewhere interesting, so I began to follow him.

Little Turtle stopped and turned to me. His shoulders squared and his eyes looked directly into mine. The training cloth was clenched in his closed fist. I stopped in my tracks.

"*Tawts*, Golden Sun," said Little Turtle in a praising voice. He softened his body and allowed me to walk over to him. I stopped a few paces away, waiting for his next command.

Just then a group of children came over, carrying wooden sticks and a leather ball. They were inviting Little Turtle to join their game. Little Turtle ran to get Pale Moon, and they went off eagerly with the strange children, leaving me hobbled at the campsite. I stamped my hind legs irritably, annoyed at being left behind.

As I stood there feeling sorry for myself, a commotion across the river caught my eye. A slender spotted filly was running loose among the tents, the rein of her bridle trailing on the ground. Many people had abandoned their work to catch her, but she dodged quick as a swallow around their outstretched hands.

I tossed my head and bounced up and down on my hind legs, wishing I could run with her.

But the hobbles held me fast. I could only watch as the filly dodged among the campfires and children's toys scattered in the grass.

Then a harsh voice rang out across the valley. "Get back here, you cowardly horse!" A man in dirty buckskin leggings decorated with tattered crow feathers was striding toward her. The filly swerved and bolted in a panic toward the riverbank, away from the sound.

As the man drew closer, the filly champed her teeth nervously and backed toward the water. She squealed and reared as she felt the cold spray behind her. The man was almost close enough to touch her now. I noticed that he held a braided quirt in one hand. The muscles in his arm bulged as though he was planning to use it.

The filly stepped back onto one of the

wooden platforms over the river. The poles were sturdy, but they were not meant to hold a horse and they groaned under the weight. The filly shuddered, and the man stepped forward.

This was the end, then. There was no way she could avoid capture.

But I was wrong. As the man reached out a rough hand toward her bridle, the filly turned and plunged off the edge of the platform into the swirling water.

A Trade and a Promise

The filly was swept away like so much dandelion fluff on the current. I neighed shrilly as she disappeared under the water. But even if I had been free, there was nothing I could have done. How could the foolish filly not have known that jumping into the water meant likely death?

The man who had driven the filly into the river seemed not to know what to do. One hand still fingered the handle of his quirt. He finally shrugged and said something in a harsh, joking tone of voice. But no one laughed. Men and women glared at him from all sides.

Just then a cry arose from downriver. I spun around to look. To my amazement, the filly was scrambling ashore in the rocky shallows on my side of the river, about a quarter mile downstream. She must not have been injured badly, because she immediately bolted upstream, once again evading people's attempts to catch her.

Her eyes were glassy and wild, and she seemed too panicked to know where she was going.

As she drew closer, I realized she was headed straight for my camp. Little Turtle's aunt and uncle had just arrived at the falls this morning and were setting up their tepee frame a short distance away. The filly crashed right through the poles and sent them flying. Blood and water streamed from her body as she raced toward where I stood.

Underneath the grime, her coat was white with splashes like black raindrops across her entire body. Her mane and tail were black. She had been badly cut by the sharp rocks in the river, and I could see pale remnants of older scars on her coat.

I backed up nervously as the filly approached on thundering hooves. I was clumsy in the hobbles and could not get out of the way. I was afraid she might crash right into me, but she came to a shuddering halt a shadow's length away.

She was close enough that I could feel her

breath whooshing over me. Her ribs showed beneath her sodden fur, and her mane and tail were tangled with burrs. From her small size I guessed she was just two winters old and had not been fed well during either of them.

The angry man, whom I had come to think of as Dirty Crow Feather, had crossed the river in a canoe. Now he strode over to where we stood, slapping his quirt against his thigh. Sitting Bear came forward to meet him, putting one hand on my neck to calm me. He stretched his other hand toward the filly, but she flinched away. Then Little Turtle's father looked more closely at the filly's spotted coat.

"No two *Maamin* are marked alike," he murmured, "and I recognize that filly, for I bred her." He looked up accusingly at Dirty Crow Feather. "She is the filly who was stolen from her dam's side in the dead of night two winters ago! I do not know if you are the thief who stole her, but judging from her condition you clearly do not know what to do with a well-bred horse once you have one."

Sitting Bear's voice was harsh, and angry sparks danced in his eyes. Dirty Crow Feather only scowled. "I'm no thief," he said. "I won that filly in a game of Bowl and Dice." His shifting body and darting eyes made me think of a guilty dog who had taken a piece of venison while its owner's back was turned.

Sitting Bear looked at the man for a long time, then went into his tent and came out with a finely carved tobacco pipe. He offered it to Dirty Crow Feather. "I will give you this in exchange for the filly," he said.

The man scowled and grabbed the pipe. "You're welcome to her," he said. He called back over his shoulder as he began to stalk away, "That filly is a good-for-nothing runaway!"

I understood that a trade had been made, and I turned to nudge the filly in welcome. She started at my touch and skittered sideways out of reach.

Don't be afraid, I said. *Now you are a* Nimi'ipuu *horse, and you don't have to go back to that cruel man.*

The filly stood glassy-eyed beside me with her ribs heaving, and I began to wonder if she had even heard me.

I do not trust men, she said finally. *The one who chased me stole me from my dam while I still needed her milk for nourishment. He rode me before I was fully grown, so that my legs and back ached. He kept me tied close to his tepee, so I could not forage for grass to keep my belly full.*

No one in Little Turtle's tribe is like that, I

reassured her, *and the other horses will welcome you into our herd.*

I have no herd, she said, and turned her back on me.

Little Turtle and Pale Moon had just returned from their game. Pale Moon took one look at the spotted filly and her eyes shone. She took a handful of dried huckleberries from a pouch around her waist and walked over to us. But the filly backed away and hid behind me.

Well, if she was going to be that way . . .

I reached out eagerly to gobble the berries instead. Pale Moon patted me as I ate them, but her eyes were trained on the filly. Pale Moon's father, Red Cloud, came over to see what all the fuss was about. Pale Moon turned to him eagerly.

"Father," she said, "this filly somehow makes my heart feel lighter. I think she is meant to take Foxtail's place."

"She looks skittish and underfed," said Red Cloud. "I have many finer horses in my herd. But if you have chosen each other, I will not argue."

He said to Sitting Bear, "I have an extra buffalo overcoat among my supplies. Would you take it in exchange for the filly?"

Sitting Bear nodded, and Red Cloud went into his tepee. He returned holding a furry robe, which he handed to Sitting Bear.

The filly had been standing beside me, watching the exchange with wary eyes. As the coat was handed over, she squealed and spun around, nearly knocking Pale Moon off her feet. She only ran a stone's throw away, then stopped and hung her head sullenly.

Traded again! she said. *I told you men can't be trusted.*

No, it is good that you were traded to Pale Moon's family, I told her. *Pale Moon is a friend of Little Turtle, and she will be a friend to you also.*

I knew what the filly's reply was going to be even before she said it.

I have no friends.

Fine, I said, frustrated by the filly's suspicious nature. *But you had better stop acting up like that. You could have hurt Pale Moon.*

She looks fine, the filly said sourly. Pale Moon had dusted herself off and was walking toward us with her hand outstretched.

"Dancing Feather," she called out in a

singsong voice. "*Tawts,* Dancing Feather, I won't hurt you."

Dancing Feather! I said. *That is your new name.*

I want no name.

Now I, too, was beginning to wonder if Pale Moon's father would have been better off with his buffalo robe, and Sitting Bear would have been wiser to keep his pipe. This filly was impossible! But I reminded myself that she was only mistrustful because she had been treated badly. As Pale Moon tried to coax the wary filly to come close enough that she could stroke her nose, I promised myself that I would help Dancing Feather feel at home among the *Nimi'ipuu.*

4

Training

When the *Nat'soxiwal* salmon run drew to a close, the *Nimi'ipuu* traded many of our horses to the other tribes gathered at the falls. The remaining horses pulled travois packed with the dried salmon, shells, baskets, and tools the *Nimi'ipuu* had received in exchange.

Soon we were herded to the highlands, where we grazed in meadows of lush grass. The women dug for roots and picked berries while the men hunted deer. Little Turtle and Pale Moon were kept busy gathering food with their families, but they worked with us whenever they could.

At first Dancing Feather resisted every effort by horse or human to befriend her. If one of the old mares tried to tell her a *Nimi'ipuu* story, Dancing Feather laid back her ears and turned disdainfully away. If Pale Moon brought her a handful of sweet blackberries, she nipped the girl's hand greedily as she took them.

Gradually the filly's ribby frame filled out and her spotted coat became sleek and glossy. Her long black tail remained a tangle of burrs, however, because she would kick anyone who approached her hindquarters too closely.

Pale Moon was very patient with her. Although Dancing Feather was a year older than I, she did not try to ride the filly. She spoke to her softly, rewarding her with praise for accepting a touch without biting. Little Turtle continued to work with me as well, teaching me to listen for his cues and focus on his intention so that we could communicate without words.

One autumn morning, Little Turtle led me to a stream to drink. The ground had frosted over the previous night, and the path sparkled in the morning light. Pale Moon was already standing at the riverbank with her hands on her hips, glaring at Dancing Feather.

"I know you are thirsty," she said. "Why won't you drink?"

"Watch," said Little Turtle. He crouched down by the stream and took a sip from his cupped hand. Then he stepped back a few paces so I could walk to the water's edge.

Since Little Turtle had taken a drink, I knew there was no danger nearby and it was safe for me to drink also. I lowered my head and took a swallow of water. It was so cold it felt like ice coating my throat, reminding me that winter was fast approaching.

Pale Moon crouched down to take a drink, too, and waited to see what Dancing Feather would do. The filly eyed the girl uncertainly, then lowered her head to drink. It was a small gesture, but it meant that Dancing Feather accepted Pale Moon as her leader. I was glad the filly was beginning to find peace and friendship among us.

When the nights grew cold and our breath began to steam in the air, the tribe moved to our winter camp in the valley between two mountains. As a cold wind blew across the campsite, I thought how lucky Little Turtle and his family were to have snug lodges to sleep in.

My coat soon grew thick and shaggy to protect me from the weather. The horses crowded close for warmth at night, but Dancing Feather always stood shivering apart from the herd.

One night, I heard a terrible howl, followed by a horse's whinny. People came running from their tents. In the murky darkness I could see the shadowy bulk of Dancing Feather standing over some dead animal on the ground. I edged closer and saw that it was a coyote, its mouth flecked with foam. The animal had been stricken with the illness that made animals lose their senses and attack without warning.

That was very brave, Sparrow said to Dancing Feather. *A mad coyote could have killed one of the weanling foals.*

Dancing Feather only twitched her tail indifferently as Pale Moon checked her body for injuries, but I saw a proud glint in her eye. After that, she did not stray so far from the herd. She would sometimes join the other mares as they stood scraping the tender inner bark from a cedar tree.

By *Latit'al*, the season of new blooms, Dancing Feather would let Pale Moon stroke her body without kicking or flinching away. She would lift her hooves on command and come running when Pale Moon whistled. I was proud of her.

Little Turtle and Pale Moon began to prepare us for riding. They laid blankets across our backs to get us used to carrying weight, and put bridles with braided leather bits in our mouths.

I didn't much like the feeling of the bit pressing on my tongue, but Dancing Feather hated it. The first time Pale Moon put the bridle on, she reared and snapped the woven rein of the bridle. Pale Moon patiently mended the bridle and tried again. By midsummer, Dancing Feather wore all her tack without fuss.

One morning, I felt a charge of excitement in the air. Somehow I knew that today was the day. I paced the campsite impatiently while

Little Turtle sat in the sweat lodge and then took his morning swim in the river.

Little Turtle and Pale Moon gathered the day's firewood and helped their mothers prepare breakfast. They always had so many chores to do before they could play with us. Finally Little Turtle put on my bridle and led me down to the stream. Pale Moon followed with Dancing Feather.

I was too excited to drink, but that wasn't what Little Turtle had in mind. He led me right into the water. Pale Moon tried to follow with Dancing Feather, but the filly squealed as the water touched her hooves, and she leaped back onto solid ground. She still remembered her terrifying encounter with the river last year.

"Starting a horse in water is a good trick

to keep them from bucking, but I don't think it will work for Dancing Feather," Pale Moon said. She patted the nervous filly and held her at the edge of the stream.

Little Turtle led me forward until I was standing chest-deep in the water. The rocks shifted under my feet, and I splashed around until I found a comfortable place to stand. It was a hot summer morning, and the cool water felt nice.

Little Turtle waded over to my side and swung his leg up over my back. I started in surprise, but I couldn't go far in the deep water. It felt strange to know that Little Turtle was on my back but not to be able to see him. I could hear his voice, though. He spoke reassuringly and leaned forward to stroke my neck. I decided this wasn't so different from having him lead me. Now I would be able to win races for Little Turtle and carry him on hunting trips.

Little Turtle pressed his heels into my sides. Despite my intentions to behave well, I balked at the pressure and backed up. Little Turtle squeezed again and tapped his leather quirt lightly against my flank.

I jumped forward, startled, and water splashed against my belly. Little Turtle took the pressure away and praised me. Now I understood that a squeeze meant I should move forward. The next time he gave the cue, I sloshed through the water and up the bank of the stream. Once I was on solid ground, Little Turtle's weight felt even stranger on my back.

I broke into a nervous jog to escape the unfamiliar feeling. I felt Little Turtle's seat bouncing on my back, which made me want to gallop and buck! I trotted faster. Then I felt pressure on the corners of my mouth. I didn't like this. I shook my head and kept trotting. The pressure got stronger.

"*Whoa*, Golden Sun," said Little Turtle.

I knew *whoa*, because Little Turtle used this command when we played the leading game. I stopped.

"*Tawts*, Golden Sun," said Little Turtle, praising me. He slid down from my back and patted my neck. I wished we could ride more, but Sitting Bear called Little Turtle away to skin a rabbit for the family's supper.

* * *

Little Turtle continued to train me whenever he had a moment between his chores. It was months before I responded naturally to small shifts in my rider's weight or the tone of his voice. But eventually we were like one creature galloping across the plains. I could feel Little Turtle's joy as we skimmed across the grass, scattering jackrabbits and racing the shadows of birds flying above.

Dancing Feather was learning also. Pale Moon had first mounted her on solid ground shortly after my first ride with Little Turtle. Dancing Feather had behaved well, although her ears flicked nervously the whole time. It seemed as though she was just waiting for some undeserved punishment. Pale Moon did not even carry a quirt. She used only her gentle

voice and pressure on the bridle to signal
Dancing Feather.

Other boys and girls in the tribe had their
own horses, too. All of them thought their
colt or filly was the bravest and fastest. The
children often challenged each other to games

and races on horseback. Our riders galloped us in circles, trying to throw spears through wooden hoops. They slipped sideways on our backs so their bodies were hidden behind our necks and pretended to shoot arrows at each other. They had weaving races through lines of rocks spaced on the ground.

Little Turtle's patient training had paid off. Some of the children's horses balked and fussed when they had to make tight turns. Sometimes they even bucked. But I knew how to sense the slightest shifts in Little Turtle's weight and adjust my strides to match. I frequently won the agility races.

Dancing Feather often became overexcited during these games. Pale Moon had to ride her away from the other horses, trotting her in slow spirals until she calmed down. Pale Moon's father sometimes shook his head and said, "That filly is as fussy as a toddler cutting its teeth!"

But when Dancing Feather was focused, she was fleet as a deer. None of the other children's horses could win a race against her. Pale

Moon's eldest brother, almost old enough to be a warrior, challenged her to a race one day. His prized black stallion, Crow, had been on many buffalo hunts and enemy raids.

Dancing Feather's hooves flashed quicker than snake strikes on the ground as they ran. She took nearly two strides for every one of Crow's. By the time the galloping horses reached the tree that marked the finish line, Dancing Feather had edged ahead by a nose and won the race.

The green leaves of *Taya'al* faded to gold, and the *Nimi'ipuu* returned to the river for the late salmon run. When the salmon had gone, we journeyed once more to the valley lodges.

Another winter passed and turned to

spring. Little Turtle was eleven now. He had gotten stronger and taller in the last year. His legs hung farther down my sides, and his seat was heavier on my back. His father sometimes let him take me out on overnight hunting trips.

I had changed, too. My slender body filled out and grew muscular. I could gallop faster and longer, and I knew what Little Turtle was going to signal almost before he asked. We weren't always in harmony—one day a snake slithered across my path and spooked me. I spun around and sent Little Turtle tumbling to the ground. But most of the time, Little Turtle and I were like one being when we rode. We were growing up together, and I wondered where our life's journey would bring us next.

Earth Medicine

As the boys and girls in the tribe grew older, they began to develop skills that would define their place in the tribe as adults. If a girl was a talented weaver, she was encouraged to make storage baskets and beautifully patterned hemp bags for her family. Some boys were excellent shots with a bow and arrow, and spent their time hunting difficult game like deer and elk. The bravest boys might even join their fathers on the long journey to hunt buffalo on the plains.

The horses of the tribe had their unique talents, too. Dancing Feather could win any race she set her mind to. Fire Tail was a brave buffalo horse who could evade the charge of an angry bull while his rider drove the stampeding herd off a cliff. Sparrow was safe and gentle for even the youngest children to ride, and her filly Winter Shadow was one of the most beautiful *Maamin* the tribe had ever seen. Her pale silver coat was powdered with white like snow on a frozen river.

At times I felt I had no abilities that set me apart. I was agile but not especially fast, and sometimes I couldn't help but spook at things. What special quality did I have that made me valuable to the tribe?

Little Turtle, however, was beginning to discover his own path. Lately he had been spending a lot of time with his grandfather, Wise Elm, who was the tribe's healer.

If a baby had a cough or a warrior broke a bone falling from his horse, Wise Elm knew what plants to use as a remedy.

Little Turtle began to take me out with Wise Elm and his spotted bay mare, River Rock, to gather herbs. River Rock had been Wise Elm's mount for more than twenty winters. Her muzzle was gray, and one of her eyes was blind and milky blue. She knew the human words for most of the plants we encountered.

Horses are born with natural instincts for what plants to eat when they suffer coughs or stomach cramps, but River Rock had learned much from Wise Elm during her many years with him.

The earth is full of medicine, she told me. *Green plants and pale roots and colorful flowers all hold the power to heal many sicknesses. Knowing how to use them correctly can mean the difference between life and death for a horse or a human.*

Sometimes we journeyed for days or even weeks to find a particular plant that Wise Elm needed.

That is hawthorn, River Rock said one day as our riders halted us near a thorny shrub with white flowers and an unpleasant smell of decay. *Its berries strengthen a weak heart.*

That is kinnikinnick, she said on another occasion while Little Turtle and Wise Elm paused to gather a plant with delicate pink bell-shaped flowers. *The dried leaves are used in smoking ceremonies, and a woman or mare who has recently given birth can be bathed in a kinnikinnick mixture to prevent infection.*

Wise Elm often spoke to Little Turtle as we rode, and I wondered if the old healer was telling the same things to my rider. One day, Wise Elm brought us to a high plateau filled with tall, bristly plants. Cream-colored seedpods grew in clusters at the top.

That is yucca, said River Rock. *A poultice*

*of the crushed roots is good for sprains and
bruises.*

Wise Elm and Little Turtle spent the day
gathering yucca leaves and roots for their
medicine stores. I dozed sleepily throughout
the afternoon, occasionally cocking a curious
ear toward a lizard scuttling through the
underbrush.

Suddenly Little Turtle cried out in alarm.
A moment later a snake came winding around
my hooves, spooking me. I snorted through
flared nostrils and edged close to River Rock,
who only flicked a curious ear in the snake's
direction. I knew snakes usually would not
attack unless you bothered them, but I didn't
like the way they slithered up underfoot with
hardly a warning.

"At least I didn't get bitten," Little Turtle called to Wise Elm from amid the yucca. "It's a good thing, too. . . . That was a rattlesnake! It's strange, though. I have been encountering snakes a lot recently."

"Maybe they have something to tell you," said Wise Elm.

"What could a snake have to tell me?" said Little Turtle. "I think I just have bad luck."

"The snake is not always bad luck," replied Wise Elm. "Brother rattlesnake has many lessons. He can teach us to keep our thoughts from wandering and to watch the path ahead of us; one misstep with an absent mind and he will strike. He can teach us to act swiftly and calmly in an emergency.

Snake, along with owl and bear, is among the most powerful of the shaman's guides."

"Yes, Grandfather," said Little Turtle, but he sounded unconvinced. He still looked shaken from his encounter with the snake.

When we got back to the camp, Wise Elm watched as Little Turtle made the yucca into a poultice for an old woman whose joints were swollen and painful. Little Turtle simmered the cleaned roots in water until they were soft, then chopped them finely and strained them through a cloth.

"Always remember that a healer can do much harm with a false remedy or a poorly prepared one," Wise Elm said. "*Hun-ya-wat* has provided us with the means to cure our illnesses, but nature also contains poisons to trick a healer who is ignorant or prideful."

Little Turtle held out a spoonful of the boiled yucca for Wise Elm's inspection, and the healer nodded with approval. I was glad that Little Turtle was learning to help the sick people and animals in the tribe. My heart felt proud and my hooves were light as I journeyed with him through the mountains and valleys to find roots and herbs for Wise Elm's medicine stores.

Little Turtle also spent many evenings in Wise Elm's tepee learning the shaman's way. I did not know what to make of the smoke and drums and chanting. Sometimes I wished I understood humans as well as Little Turtle understood horses.

But despite the mysteries that remained

to me about men and their medicine, I had learned much from my time with the old healer. If a horse in the tribe felt the cramping pain of colic, I knew to direct him to a patch of chicory, meadowsweet, or peppermint. For coughs, I advised nibbling on horehound leaves. If a mare had a difficult birth, black cherry bark or kinnikinnick would restore her strength and prevent infection. If it was time for a foal to be weaned but the colt would not stop trying to nurse, I urged the mare to eat sage to make her milk bitter.

When I looked at a filly whose runny nose had cleared thanks to my advice, or saw a stallion whose cut fetlock had healed because of a poultice Little Turtle had prepared, I felt pride in my heart.

When I saw Dancing Feather cantering
through the blue camas fields with Pale Moon,
I was joyful also. It was nearing *Tustimasat'al*,
the moon of ripe berries, and the world seemed
full of health and healing.

But as many things do, this was soon to
change.

6

Broken Trust

It was time for the camas harvest, and dozens of *Nimi'ipuu* women were kneeling among the wilting flowers, digging up the pale bulbs with sharpened sticks. Serviceberries were heavy on the bushes, and Pale Moon and Little Turtle rode us to a patch that grew half a day's journey from camp.

As I was nosing through the grass looking for fallen berries, I heard Little Turtle cry out in pain. I spun around to see what was the matter, then shied as a striped snake slithered through the grass near my hooves. Dancing Feather saw my fear and dove forward to chase the snake away. I snorted my thanks.

Little Turtle held up his hand as Pale Moon came running over to see what was the matter. Two beads of blood welled from punctures on his skin.

"Did you see what kind of snake bit you?" asked Pale Moon, looking worried.

"Yes, it was just a garter snake. It snapped at my wrist as I was reaching for some fallen berries. I must have disturbed its afternoon nap."

Little Turtle shrugged and wrapped a deerskin bandage around his arm. *Nimi'ipuu* children were taught to bear their injuries without complaint. Still, I noticed my rider wincing from time to time as he continued gathering berries.

"Snakes again," said Little Turtle. "A snake spooked Golden Sun when I was out gathering yucca just a few weeks ago."

"Well," said Pale Moon, "there are a lot of snakes."

"Yes, I guess that's true," Little Turtle said. "Wise Elm said it might be a sign, but I don't know what these snakes could have to tell me. Personally, I would prefer if they just minded their own business!"

When their hemp bags were full, Little Turtle and Pale Moon climbed onto our backs. They passed the journey home by singing and telling stories as they rode. I couldn't understand the words to the stories, but I liked the songs because I could make the rhythm of my hooves match the music of Little Turtle's voice.

"I'll race you to the tree on top of that hill," Pale Moon said suddenly. She pointed to a cedar tree on the horizon. "Don't spill your berries!"

Without waiting for a reply, Pale Moon kicked Dancing Feather into a gallop. Little Turtle leaned forward and urged me after her with his voice.

I quickened my pace until I drew up alongside Dancing Feather. She flattened her ears nervously. I was caught up in the joy of running, and I reached out to nip her playfully. *Catch me if you can,* I cried, bolting forward and leaving her in the dust. I snorted and lengthened my stride as we drew closer to the tree on the hill. We might just win a race for once!

Then I heard hoofbeats behind me. Dancing Feather came flying past us, her black mane whipping back so that it mingled with Pale Moon's hair. My heart and my hooves pounded like thunder as I tried to keep pace with her.

But hard as I ran, she was faster. Dancing Feather passed the tree a length ahead of me. Pale Moon whooped with triumph and raised an arm above her head.

Dancing Feather dropped her head suddenly and began to buck. Her heels flashed in the air, and Pale Moon went flying from her back. Dancing Feather took off at a gallop across the prairie. Soon she disappeared over the crest of a hill, leaving only a lazy cloud of dust in her wake.

Little Turtle drew me to a halt and jumped down from my back. He dropped my rein and left me ground-tied as he hurried over to Pale Moon. "Stand, Golden Sun," he said firmly.

My instinct was to run after Dancing Feather. I didn't want to be left behind! But Little Turtle had given me a command, and I would not break his trust like Dancing Feather had broken Pale Moon's.

"Are you all right?" asked Little Turtle as he knelt by Pale Moon.

"Dancing Feather ran away!" said Pale Moon. She looked as though she was about to cry.

"I will find her later," said Little Turtle. "But now you must tell me if you are hurt anywhere."

Pale Moon's right wrist was already very swollen, and she winced as Little Turtle touched it. "I think it is broken," she said. Her voice was steady, but her eyes shone with pain.

Little Turtle searched the ground until he saw a straight stick lying under the tree that had marked the end of our race. He cut away the bark with his knife. Then he unwrapped the bandage from his own wrist and tied the splint around Pale Moon's arm.

Little Turtle helped her up onto my back.
I tried to walk as smoothly as possible so as
not to cause Pale Moon further pain.

When Little Turtle and I returned to
search for Dancing Feather, we spotted her
standing forlornly in a sandy hollow some
distance from camp, her head hanging low.

Why did you buck like that? I asked her, laying back my ears as we approached. *You hurt Pale Moon!*

I couldn't help myself, she said. *I know that Pale Moon would not hurt me, but when she raised her arm I felt such fear in my heart that my hooves would not listen to my head.*

I only snorted in response. Little Turtle leaned down to tie a rope around Dancing Feather's neck. She plodded dispiritedly beside me as we walked back to camp.

When we arrived, Pale Moon's father was fashioning a new bow and arrow set nearby. He put down the mallet he was using to pound a piece of deer sinew and hurried over to us. He exchanged a few words with Little Turtle, then strode purposefully toward Dancing Feather.

The filly trembled as she eyed his hard body language. Red Cloud did not strike her, only took her by the bridle and hobbled her with his other horses, his mouth set in a grim line.

Is he going to trade me away? said Dancing Feather, tossing her head. *Will I have to leave Pale Moon?*

He might, I said. *I do not think he would keep an untrustworthy horse for his daughter.*

Dancing Feather looked so forlorn that I felt sorry for her. But I had no time to comfort her, for Little Turtle came over and climbed onto my back. Wise Elm was mounted on River Rock nearby.

Where are we going? I asked the spotted bay mare as we rode away from camp together.

To find some willow bark for Pale Moon, I

imagine, she said. *It eases the pain of sprains and broken bones.*

I know, I said. *Little Turtle gathered some just last week when Raven Song's little boy fell and hurt his leg. Little Turtle knows where to find it, so I wonder why Wise Elm is coming with us.*

I listened curiously to our riders' speech as they dismounted near a stand of willow trees.

"You have learned much about healing and medicine, Little Turtle," Wise Elm was saying. "And you acted calmly in a crisis today. It seems to me that you will soon be ready to take your vision quest."

Little Turtle bit his lip as he cut away the tough outer bark from one of the trees, then began to scrape bits of tender inner bark onto a deerskin cloth. "I am pleased you think well of my accomplishments, Grandfather," he said finally, "but I do not know if I am ready to receive a *wyakin*."

"You are eleven winters old now. Maybe it is time for you to take your place as a man in the tribe."

"Yes, Grandfather," said Little Turtle. He looked uncertain.

I recognize none of these words, I said to River Rock. *Do you?*

I know wyakin, said River Rock. *When boys and girls in the tribe reach Little Turtle's age, they go up in the mountains to seek a wyakin, an animal guide who grants them some special power. They are gone for days at a time, and they do not eat or sleep until their wyakin comes.*

This sounded frightening to me. I did not

like to think of Little Turtle alone on a storm-swept mountain.

But Little Turtle doesn't need to do this, I said. *I am the animal who journeys with him, so I must be his* wyakin.

River Rock snorted gently with laughter. *I have no doubt you are a valued friend to Little Turtle,* she said, *but you are not his* wyakin.

I still didn't understand why Little Turtle would need any animal other than me to guide him.

When we returned to camp, Little Turtle boiled the willow bark into tea for Pale Moon and made a poultice of crushed yarrow.

Pale Moon's arm healed in several weeks. She wanted to ride Dancing Feather again, but Red Cloud refused.

"The filly is dangerous," he said. "I will trade her away when we meet the Salish tribe at the fall salmon run. Last time I spoke to Runs in Shadow, he wanted a spotted mare to breed with his stallion. I think he will make a handsome offer for this filly, and you can choose any other horse in my herd."

Trade was a word that Dancing Feather and I knew well, and she twitched her tail nervously.

"Thank you for your generosity, Father," Pale Moon was saying. "But I do not want any horse in your herd, I want Dancing Feather. She is not a bad filly—she is only frightened."

"After several years in our tribe, she should have learned by now that there is nothing to be frightened of."

"Father, please," Pale Moon said. "Let me have another chance with Dancing Feather. If she misbehaves or hurts me again, you can trade her to Runs in Shadow. But please give her one more chance!"

Red Cloud looked at his daughter for a long time. "Very well," he said. "I feel there is something about that filly beyond healing, but perhaps with more patience she will develop into a trustworthy mount for my only daughter."

"Thank you, Father!" said Pale Moon. She sniffed a few times and wiped her nose on a deerskin kerchief.

"I do not like to see you crying, daughter," said Red Cloud. "Are you not happy with our agreement?"

"I am not crying, Father," said Pale Moon. "My nose has simply been running like a river these past few days. My throat is scratchy as straw. I must ask Little Turtle if he has a remedy for this. And do not worry, Father. With a little more patience, Dancing Feather will be perfect."

Red Cloud only grunted skeptically and turned back to replacing a broken pole on the family's travois.

It sounded to me like Dancing Feather was being given another chance. She walked over to nuzzle Pale Moon's shoulder, as if in apology. Pale Moon reached up between Dancing Feather's ears to smooth her forelock, and the filly gave a startled squeal and jerked her head away. Pale Moon winced as

Dancing Feather's muzzle hit her wrist. The bones had mended, but I knew the arm pained her at times, for she often asked Little Turtle to make a willow bark poultice for her at the end of a long day harvesting camas or looking after her young cousins.

I was worried about Dancing Feather. The filly had a good heart, but she often let fear rule her. I hoped she would behave more like a proper *Nimi'ipuu* horse, steadfast and loyal instead of skittish and wary. I had a feeling this was her last chance to prove she truly belonged to our tribe.

Stolen Breath

A few days later, I stood watching as Little Turtle crushed some wild gingerroot into paste. This remedy was to soothe the stomach of a young woman named Dawn Star who was expecting her first child. As Little Turtle poured hot water over the crushed ginger to make tea, a cry arose from one of the scouts on a distant hill.

We both looked up as Dancing Feather came galloping riderless into camp, her neck covered in lather. She looked the same as when I'd first laid eyes on her at the salmon falls—wild and untamed.

My heart sank. It looked as if she had run away again, and I was sure Red Cloud would trade her to the first person with so much as a sack of camas bulbs to offer.

I see you have thrown your rider again, I said angrily as Dancing Feather skidded to a halt in front of me. *Is she hurt badly?*

I didn't throw her, cried Dancing Feather, gasping for breath. *Pale Moon is ill! We went for a ride along the river, and she began to cough.*

She dismounted to take a drink from the river, but she was too weak to climb onto my back again. She fell asleep by the riverbank, and I could not wake her. Her skin felt very hot. We must go back to her at once!

Someone gave an angry cry behind us. I spun on my haunches as Red Cloud came up to Dancing Feather and seized her dangling rein. "What have you done to my daughter?" he cried, jerking roughly on the bridle.

Dancing Feather rose up on her hind legs in terror. Red Cloud struck her with his fist, and she reared still higher, slashing the air with her hooves.

Listen! I cried to her. *They will soon understand that you did not throw Pale Moon. Just calm down before you hurt someone.*

Dancing Feather dropped to all four legs and let out a shuddering breath.

Now pull away quickly before he ties you up, I said.

Dancing Feather jerked the rein from Red Cloud's hand and skittered about ten paces away. She neighed shrilly and wheeled around in a small circle.

Follow me, follow me to Pale Moon! she cried.

But Red Cloud did not understand.

"Let the horse run away," he said in disgust. "I have no time to chase down a disobedient nag when my daughter is lying injured somewhere."

But Little Turtle was watching Dancing

Feather carefully. "I don't think she is trying to run away," he said. "I think she has returned to lead us to Pale Moon."

He slipped on my bridle and swung up onto my back. Red Cloud whistled for his own horse, who came running.

We set off after Dancing Feather, who began to canter away through the valley. As worried as I was, I felt great pride that Dancing Feather had returned to find help for her rider.

As we rounded a bend in the river, I saw Pale Moon collapsed on the sharp stones at the edge of the bank. She looked as frail as a corn-husk doll. Dancing Feather trotted over and nudged her with her muzzle.

Pale Moon stirred. "Dancing Feather . . . you came back," she murmured. Then her eyes closed, and coughs racked her body. It sounded like someone was trying to steal the very breath from her body.

Red Cloud dismounted and lifted her onto his bay stallion. Dance with Arrows was normally fiery and difficult to manage, but today he walked quietly with Pale Moon slumped on his back. Little Turtle and I rode close beside them to keep Pale Moon from falling.

When we got back to camp, Red Cloud carried Pale Moon into the family's tepee and called on Wise Elm for guidance. The old healer gathered his herbs, feathers, and shaman's drums and went into Pale Moon's tent. For many hours, the sounds of chanting and drums came from within.

Dancing Feather was beside herself with worry, tossing her head as she paced the campsite.

You did not abandon your rider in a time of need, I said to her. *You are a true* Nimi'ipuu *horse*.

The concern did not ease from Dancing Feather's eyes. *I only hope my help did not come too late*, she said.

To my surprise, Red Cloud came over to comfort Dancing Feather during a moment he was not with Pale Moon. Dancing Feather's eyes widened fearfully at first, but she lowered her head when she realized he was only trying to stroke her neck. I was glad Red Cloud understood that Dancing Feather had not hurt Pale Moon.

But despite Wise Elm's efforts, Pale Moon's cough did not improve. She lay coughing and murmuring feverishly in her tepee for nearly a week. Worry hung over the campsite like a dark cloud.

Do you think Pale Moon will die? I asked River Rock. I was standing on the side of her blind eye, and I nudged the old mare gently so she would know where I was.

I do not know, said River Rock. *Dancing Feather said that Pale Moon's skin felt hot. When a horse's skin gets very hot, something is wrong inside.*

I felt a chill that had little to do with the cold autumn breeze. Little Turtle came over to Wise Elm, who was boiling some strong-smelling herbs over the fire nearby.

"Grandfather," he said. "I think it is time for me to seek my *wyakin*."

Wise Elm's face was as lined and solemn as an ancient tree that had weathered many storms. "It is late in the year, Little Turtle," he said. "You would risk freezing in the mountains."

"I must go ask for guidance so I can help Pale Moon."

"You have already helped her. We have given her medicine from the plants you gathered last summer. Speedwell to help her cough up the fluid in her lungs, and coltsfoot to ease the irritation in her chest. We have said prayers for her. We have done all we can. If it is the will of *Hun-ya-wat*, she will recover."

"Maybe it is the will of *Hun-ya-wat* that I seek guidance from my guardian spirits on her behalf."

Wise Elm looked at Little Turtle for a long time. "It seems just yesterday that you were a little boy sneaking honey from my medicine stores whenever my back was turned. I see you are now becoming a man. If you feel your *wyakin* is ready to reveal itself to you, then you must take this journey."

"*Tawts*, Grandfather," said Little Turtle. His eyes shone with a brightness I had never seen before.

That evening, he went into the sweat lodge and stayed there all night. His mother and elder sister brought water to pour over the hot stones. When Little Turtle emerged the next dawn, he wore only a loincloth and his body was smeared with white paint. Wise Elm stood near my shoulder as Little Turtle drew near. He handed Little Turtle a buffalo robe.

"May *Hun-ya-wat* speak to you through his creation."

Little Turtle started to walk away, and I followed him eagerly.

"Stay, Golden Sun," he said. He was not holding the training cloth, but his hands and his voice told me to be still. He began to walk away again.

I whinnied with distress. I knew what *stay* meant, but Little Turtle was going somewhere important and I wanted to go with him. It is a very serious thing for a horse to break his rider's command, but at that moment I couldn't help myself. I cantered over to him as he reached the edge of camp.

"Golden Sun, you must stay here," said Little Turtle. "It will be very cold in the mountains. There may be danger." His face was calm, but a flicker of uncertainty showed in his eyes.

Then Wise Elm spoke. "Normally a boy goes on his vision quest alone, but I do not think even hobbles would stop this horse from following you."

"And I would much rather have him with me!" said Little Turtle. He sprang onto my back and turned me north to the mountains. I broke into an eager trot, my hooves clattering on the frozen earth. I did not know where we were going, but I knew this was no ordinary ride.

Vision Quest

Little Turtle sat tall and quiet on my back as he guided me toward the mountain looming on the horizon. The air grew thin and cold as we began to climb, and the soil turned to rock beneath my hooves. Soon the only thing above us was sky.

When we reached the highest point on the mountain, Little Turtle slid down from my back. Then he piled loose stones into a pyramid and placed a hawk's feather from his medicine bag at the peak. He sat down with his back against the rocks and closed his eyes.

For a day and a night and a day again, Little Turtle sat motionless. Sometimes his lips moved softly, but I could not hear his words. The sweeping cold seemed to pierce right through my thick fur into my bones, and I wondered how Little Turtle could stand it. I was thankful that he had the buffalo robe to shelter him from the worst of the elements.

I stood so my body shielded Little Turtle from the wind, but his lips remained shadowy blue. Frost beaded in his wind-tangled hair, streaking it white as though he had become the oldest of men.

The sun's rays melted the rime soon after dawn, but it felt like my bones had barely begun to warm before the light faded again. Night falls fast in the mountains, and it seemed the sun had hardly blazed bloodshot red on the horizon before it crashed down somewhere behind the mountains and the world fell into icy shadow once more.

I feared for Little Turtle. He mumbled hoarsely to no one, and a glistening sweat broke out on his brow despite the cold. I stayed close to him through a third cold night and prayed for morning. Even the stars seemed to glint like they had frozen in the sky. After endless ages, they began to fade with the coming dawn and the sky turned milky gray.

Yet still, the sun did not rise. I wondered if the world would remain gray forever and no sun would rise again to warm the frost from my back or from Little Turtle's bowed head.

Then I heard a dry rattling sound that sent a chill through my body. I sensed motion near my feet. A green and black rattlesnake was winding its way around my hooves. The air surrounding it seemed to shimmer, and I could not have said whether it was a snake or only a dream.

I wanted to strike out a hoof and crush it, but my legs felt so heavy and my mind was so fuzzy that I only stood dumbly and watched it slither across the rock toward Little Turtle. I managed to snort in warning, and Little Turtle looked up and saw the snake.

His eyes widened, but he did not budge as the snake moved toward him. It stopped near Little Turtle's feet, lifting its head and flicking out its forked tongue to taste the air.

At that moment, the first rays of morning light pierced through the clouds on the horizon. Little Turtle and the snake locked gazes, and the only motion was the flutter of the snake's red tongue. The light kept getting stronger, until it seemed like the sun had expanded to fill the whole world.

It was then that the snake spoke. The languages of horses and of snakes and of humans are normally separate things, but for a moment on that lonely mountain they were one. And the snake said to Little Turtle:

You are a healer, and I will be your guide.

I grant you the power to draw the poison of sickness from human or animal.

Pale Moon's cure is the root of the kouse plant, and I will share with you a healing song to call her wandering spirit back to her body.

The snake lowered its head and began to move across the rock. It traced a path like two circles flowing into each other without end. The whole world was full of the snake's song. It rattled like dead leaves scraping the earth. It piped like the call of a newly hatched chick. It flowed like the sound of water running over stones.

The snake coiled in front of Little Turtle, and the song faded. Little Turtle whistled the song back to the snake through parched lips. "Thank you," he whispered.

Then the snake turned its head to me and its dark eyes glittered. I took a few nervous steps back.

Horse, you are a healer, too, said the snake, and then slipped away through a crevice in the rock. The golden light faded, and Little Turtle and I were alone in another pale mountain dawn.

Little Turtle got to his feet. Though his face was lined with exhaustion, his eyes were clear and bright. He came over and rested his head against my neck, breathing soft words of thanks into my ear. Then he slid onto my back and whistled the snake's song into the cold air as we began the long journey home.

Two Healers

Little Turtle rode me down the face of the mountain until we reached the path we had taken from the *Nimi'ipuu* camp. I headed eagerly toward home, looking forward to food and safety and rest. But Little Turtle reined me in the other direction.

"We can't go home yet, Golden Sun," he said, laying a hand on my neck. "I know Wise Elm's medicine stores like the back of my hand, and he does not have any kouse root. We will have to find some ourselves."

I didn't understand his words, but I realized our journey was not yet over. I pushed thoughts of golden maize and dried berries out of my mind as Little Turtle urged me forward and began to guide me along a steep ridge. Small stones showered down the face of a rocky cliff below. I could see the bones of a less fortunate animal, who had fallen or been chased over the edge. Although I was very tired, I paid close attention to where I set my hooves; one misstep would be our last.

Several times a quick shift in Little Turtle's

weight alerted me that I was getting too close to the edge. Without my rider, I would have probably stumbled in my fatigue and gone tumbling over the cliff.

The sun was high above us when we reached a clearing where the ground leveled off a little. A stream trickled away down the rocky slope. I recognized the place from our travels with Wise Elm.

A stand of kouse plants normally grew here. In the summertime they were tall flowers with bright yellow blossoms, but all the plants had withered and turned brown in the cold. It was impossible to tell one from another. The precious kouse root could be buried anywhere in the stony soil.

Little Turtle got down on his hands and

knees and began to dig. I lowered my head and sniffed the dried-up vegetation. My senses were keener than Little Turtle's, but all I smelled was dirt.

I scraped my hoof along the ground in frustration. If Little Turtle could not find the kouse, what good would his *wyakin*'s advice be? As I continued to paw the dirt, my hoof struck a root. I smelled something sharp and bitter, like wild parsley.

I knew the scent of kouse root! I continued to paw until the pale wrinkled root was exposed. I whinnied to Little Turtle, who hurried over to where I stood.

"You've found it, Golden Sun!" he cried. He bent down and cut a large piece from the root with his obsidian knife. He brushed off

the dirt and put the root in his medicine bag. Then he sprang up onto my back again.

I traveled along the treacherous ridge as quickly as I dared. When we reached the valley floor, I broke into a gallop.

We arrived at the *Nimi'ipuu* camp by sunset. Little Turtle jumped off my back, leaving my rein trailing on the ground. He called out for Wise Elm, and the old healer emerged from one of the lodges. His face was creased where it must have been resting against a folded blanket.

"I am glad to see you return safely, Little Turtle," said Wise Elm. "But I'm afraid Pale Moon is no better. I have quieted her cough a little with licorice tea, but this has done nothing to cure her sickness."

"My *wyakin* has guided me to a remedy for her," said Little Turtle, taking the root from his medicine bag.

"Kouse root," murmured Wise Elm. "It works well for a certain type of cough, one that often comes from tribes who have had contact with white men. I did not think Pale Moon had this illness, but perhaps I was mistaken."

Little Turtle crushed the kouse root while Pale Moon's mother brought her into the sweat lodge. Dancing Feather came and stood beside me. I told her of the cold nights on the mountain and of the snake's message for Little Turtle. I did not tell her that the snake had also called me a healer. I had only found the root by accident, after all.

Little Turtle finished preparing the medicine. "Pour hot water over this and let her breathe the steam," he said, handing Pale Moon's mother the crushed kouse root on a cloth.

Pale Moon remained in the sweat lodge overnight. My bones shook with the pounding of drums as Little Turtle's voice rose and fell in the ceremonial chants. Even over these rhythmic sounds, I could hear Pale Moon's ragged coughing.

I could not help but notice how Dancing Feather flinched every time she heard Pale Moon cough. I had begun to doubt it would ever happen, but I knew now that Dancing Feather had come to love Pale Moon as I loved Little Turtle.

Pale Moon's cough faded for a moment, and Dancing Feather closed her eyes and let her head droop toward the ground. She jerked awake as her rider suddenly choked again and gasped for breath. I nibbled Dancing Feather's shoulder gently in reassurance.

The chanting went on and on as the stars came out and glittered coldly above. The light cast by the campfire made the world seem full of living shadows. A shiver ran through me, although I felt warm and safe.

Finally the drums stopped. Silence.

Dancing Feather had been dozing, but when the noise stopped she started awake. She looked at me with wide eyes.

Do you hear that? she said.

I hear nothing, I replied.

Yes, exactly, she said. *Pale Moon isn't coughing!*

A few minutes later, Little Turtle emerged from the lodge. He looked weary. Dancing Feather and I went over to him and blew affectionate breaths across his body. He paused to stroke us for a moment before walking over to Pale Moon's mother and father, who waited anxiously nearby.

"Her fever has broken," he said, "and the sickness is gone. Give her some of the kouse root in hot water whenever she is thirsty. Her throat is still raw and sore, so if she begins to cough give her elderberry syrup dissolved in honey."

"Thank you, Little Turtle," said Red Cloud hoarsely. He looked at the boy with concern.

"I know you have had no food or sleep since you journeyed to the mountain three days ago. Eat this, and then get some rest."

He handed Little Turtle a piece of salmon pemmican. My rider gulped it down gratefully, but instead of retreating to his tepee he came back to me. He wrapped his arms around my neck and leaned his head against me.

I normally slept standing, but my legs and back ached from our trek in the mountains and the long vigil, so I dropped to my knees and lay curled on my side to sleep. Little Turtle wrapped his buffalo robe snugly around him and lay down beside me, using my body as a pillow. Though the wind blew cold that night, we were warm together as we slept under the stars.

Pale Moon was nearly well again by the time of the Winter Spirit Dance. I had learned from River Rock that this was a ceremony where everyone gathered in the lodges to speak of their vision quests.

I imagined Little Turtle telling the story of the snake who came to us on the mountain.

Maybe he would also tell of how I stayed with him through the long days and nights, how I never left his side in the wind and the cold. I did not know the words they were chanting in the lodge, but I felt the music in my bones and I understood that humans and snakes and horses could sometimes speak to each other despite their different languages.

One afternoon in early spring, Pale Moon sat stirring a basket of dried elderberries mixed with water and honey, cooking them over a hot stone she had taken from the fire. River Rock said it was medicine to ease away the last of her cough, but it smelled like a treat to me.

Do you think if we wandered close and looked very hungry, Pale Moon would give us a taste of those berries? said Dancing Feather. Long gone was the frightened filly who had refused to take food from a human hand.

Dancing Feather nosed her way toward the cooking basket, stepping carefully around a group of children playing with their stick horses near the fire. Pale Moon drizzled a little of the hot berry syrup onto a flat rock for Dancing Feather. She licked it eagerly.

"Do you think you'll be well enough to ride soon?" asked Little Turtle, coming over to the fire.

"I think so," Pale Moon replied. "My cough is much better. I guess there was a reason for you seeing snakes all year—it turns out they had something to tell you."

Little Turtle laughed. "At the time, I only thought I had bad luck."

Pale Moon's expression turned serious. "I really thought I might die from my sickness. You were very brave to go up onto that cold mountain and ask your *wyakin* for help."

Little Turtle shrugged modestly. "Well, I had Golden Sun," he said. "The nights were much less dark with a friend to keep me company."

Pale Moon smiled. "Yes, that is the way of things," she said.

Dancing Feather was still nosing around the fire looking for spilled syrup, and some of Pale Moon's little cousins came over to beg for a taste of the sweetened berries. Dancing Feather stood quietly while the children toddled around her hooves, stroking her legs and reaching up to pat her nose.

Now everyone knew that Dancing Feather would not kick the children or bite the camp dogs. She had earned back every bit of the trust she had broken, and I felt that some of the wounds less visible than those scarring her flanks had finally healed.

The next morning, Little Turtle and Pale Moon awoke before sunrise to take us for a ride. A robin trilled as we walked through the milky half-light of dawn. Soon the world would be green and alive again. Beside me, Dancing Feather pranced lightly and arched her neck, proud to carry Pale Moon once more.

I felt a glow of pride, too, as I remembered the snake's message on the mountain. I liked to think that my guidance and friendship had helped Dancing Feather, much like Little Turtle's remedies helped sick members of the tribe.

Little Turtle and Pale Moon drew us to a halt by a stream and dismounted to wash their faces and hands. Droplets glittered on their cheeks as the sun rose above the mountains in the distance.

Dancing Feather and I stepped forward and drank gratefully from the rushing stream. We stood contentedly, water streaming from our muzzles, as Little Turtle and Pale Moon turned their faces to the sky to give thanks for the new day.

APPENDIX

MORE ABOUT THE APPALOOSA

History of the Appaloosa

Appaloosas are a breed of horses with distinctive spotted coats. Although the Nez Perce tribe first developed the Appaloosa, brightly patterned horses have existed long before they were brought to the New World. Leopard-spotted horses appear in cave drawings from France dating to 18,000 BCE. A Chinese statue from around 800 BCE portrays a horse that looks a lot like a modern snowflake Appaloosa. Indeed, it could nearly be Golden Sun! Paintings and sculptures of brightly patterned horses have appeared all across Europe since at least the tenth century CE.

Spanish settlers brought horses to the Americas in the 1500s. Some of them were traded to Native American tribes. The *Nimi'ipuu*, or Nez Perce, as they were called by white settlers, probably first got horses in the early 1700s from their allies, the Cayuse. The arrival of the horse changed the Nez Perce way of life. In earlier years, the tribe had traveled on foot, using dogs as pack animals. Horses allowed the Nez Perce to expand their territory and track buffalo across the plains.

Within a few generations, the Nez Perce gained a reputation as excellent horse breeders. In 1806 Meriwether Lewis, the famous American explorer, wrote of "lofty, elegantly formed horses," some with "large spots of white irregularly scattered with . . . some other dark colour," among the tribe's herds. European settlers called them Palouse horses, after the nearby Palouse River. This term eventually became *Appaloosa*. The Nez Perce word for Appaloosa is *Maamin*. Unfortunately, many of the original *Maamin* were killed in the 1877 Nez Perce War.

The Appaloosa Today

The Appaloosa Horse Club is a registration society that was started in 1938 in an effort to preserve the breed. Registered Appaloosas can compete in breed shows and earn national points. The ApHC is a color registry, so any horse with Appaloosa coloring can be registered, even if its parents are unknown.

The ApHC recognizes five Appaloosa coat patterns: blanket, snowflake, leopard, varnish roan, and frost. Solid-colored Appaloosas can still be registered as breeding stock, but must have the breed's other characteristics: mottled skin, striped hooves, and white sclera, which is a protective membrane surrounding the eye.

Did you know you can feel an Appaloosa's spots? The skin under the white or dark

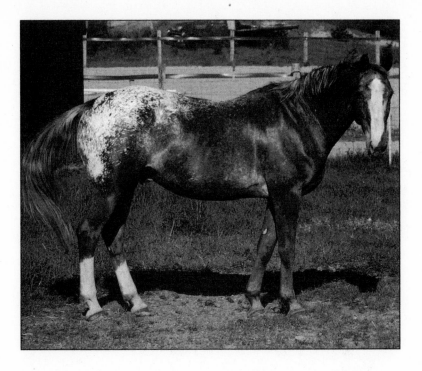

patches on an Appaloosa's coat is often raised, like a Braille tracing of the pattern.

An Appaloosa's conformation, or build, is ideally hardy and compact, with tough hooves

and sturdy legs capable of holding up to strenu-
ous ranch work. They are usually medium-sized
horses of fourteen to sixteen hands. Today there
are more than thirty-two thousand registered
Appaloosas. You can visit the Appaloosa Horse
Club's official Web site at www.appaloosa.com
to learn more about this remarkable breed.

More About the Nez Perce

The Nez Perce word for their tribe is *Nimi'ipuu*,
which simply means "the people." Their native
lands covered large areas of Idaho, Oregon,
and Washington at the time of the Lewis and
Clark expedition in 1805. The *Nimi'ipuu*'s
travels took them across mountain ranges,
rivers, and vast stretches of open prairie. The

tribe split off into smaller groups during most of the year, often holding a large reunion on the plains in the summer.

The phrase *Nez Perce* means "pierced nose" in French. This name is actually the result of a mistranslation during the expedition of Lewis and Clark. Some northwestern tribes wore decorative shells or other jewelry through their noses, but the *Nimi'ipuu* did not.

The Nez Perce lived in harmony with nature, never taking more than they needed. They traveled with the seasons. They fished for salmon in the spring and fall. Hunting parties journeyed long distances to follow the migrating buffalo, sometimes not returning for a year or more. In the winter, Nez Perce families moved to lodges in the mountains. In the summer, they dug camas and kouse roots on the plains and gathered berries and other edible plants in season.

The Nez Perce also used plants as medicine. The tribe had healers who knew what herbs should be used for certain illnesses. Nez Perce medicine men and women were also shamans, spiritual healers who learned chants and rituals to help cure a sick or injured person.

Vision Quests

When Nez Perce children were around nine to fifteen years old, they would be instructed by an elder to go on a vision quest. Both boys and girls went on vision quests. They would fast, pray, and cleanse themselves in a sweat lodge to prepare for this journey. They would smear their bodies with white paint to symbolize purity of spirit. Their journey was often to some high place, like a mountaintop. They would remain there for days to fast and pray while waiting for their *wyakin*, or spirit guide, to come to them in the form of an animal.

If the vision seeker was lucky enough to receive a *wyakin*, this animal would give the Nez Perce child some special power to use throughout his or her whole life. The snake was a powerful *wyakin* for healers and shamans.

A New Beginning

Horses have been an important part of Nez Perce culture since the 1700s. Unfortunately, many of the Appaloosas that survived the 1877 war were bred with draft horses, diminishing the refinement of the breed. In more recent years, Appaloosas were often bred with quarter horses. This cross restored quality to the breed, but created horses with different conformation than those originally bred by the *Nimi'ipuu*.

The Nez Perce Horse Project is an effort to re-create the original Nez Perce *Maamin*. Modern Appaloosas are being bred with a Central European breed called the Akhal-Teke, known for its agility and stamina. This cross has already produced a number of beautiful spotted horses with the elegance and endurance that the first *Maamin* must have possessed. You can find out more at www.nezpercehorseregistry.com.

∽ COMING SOON! ∽

Arabian Desert, Ninth Century

Yatimah is a black Arabian filly whose name means "orphan."
She enjoys her life at the oasis, with sheep to tease, other
foals to race, and the daughter of her Bedouin owner to take
care of her. But when the colt who is her foster brother is
stolen in a raid, Yatimah realizes her true birthright. Here
is Yatimah's story . . . in her own words.

About the Author

Whitney Sanderson was born and home-schooled in Ware, Massachusetts. Her family has owned horses since she was a child, and her bookshelves were always filled with horse stories. When she isn't writing, she volunteers at a horse rescue and therapeutic riding center. Whitney and her mother, who illustrated this story, have an Appaloosa named Thor, who posed as the model for Golden Sun.

About the Illustrator

Ruth Sanderson grew up with a love for horses. She drew them constantly, and her first oil painting, at age fourteen, was a horse portrait.

Ruth has illustrated and retold many fairy tales and likes to feature horses in them whenever possible. Her book about a magical horse, *The Golden Mare, the Firebird, and the Magic Ring*, won the Texas Bluebonnet Award in 2003. She illustrated the first Black Stallion paperback covers and a number of chapter books about horses, most recently *Summer Pony* and *Winter Pony* by Jean Slaughter Doty.

Ruth and her daughter have two horses, an Appaloosa named Thor and a quarter horse named Gabriel. She lives with her family in Massachusetts.

To find out more about her adventures with horses and the research she did to create the illustrations in this book, visit her Web site, www.ruthsanderson.com.

☞ Collect all the books in the ☜
Horse Diaries series!

Elska
CATHERINE HAPKA
illustrated by RUTH SANDERSON

Bell's Star
ALISON HART
illustrated by RUTH SANDERSON

Koda
PATRICIA HERMES
illustrated by RUTH SANDERSON

☞ And coming soon ☜

Maestoso Petra
JANE KENDALL
illustrated by RUTH SANDERSON

Golden Sun
WHITNEY SANDERSON
illustrated by RUTH SANDERSON

Yatimah
CATHERINE HAPKA
illustrated by RUTH SANDERSON